Bubble Buster

ALAN HORSFIELD

Illustrated by Luke Jurevicius

sundance

The Story Characters

Buster

He goes on the ride of his life.

Holly

Buster's sister.

Dad

Buster's father.

Uncle Fred

He loves his garden.

The Story Setting

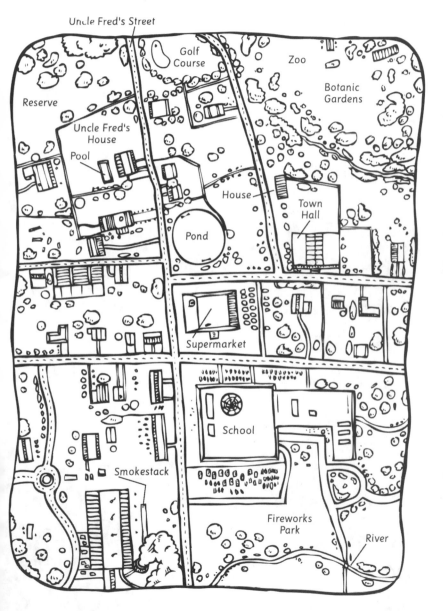

Uncle Fred's Street

Golf Course

Zoo

Botanic Gardens

Reserve

Uncle Fred's House

Pool

House

Town Hall

Pond

Supermarket

School

Smokestack

Fireworks Park

River

TABLE OF CONTENTS

CHAPTER 1

Buster and the Compost

Buster loved pool parties. He could jump and bomb. He could splash and fool around.

Buster jumped on Holly's blow-up seal. The seal burst. It hissed as it flew across the pool.

"Wow!" said Buster. But Holly was not amused. Her seal looked like an old plastic bag.

Buster dived under the water when his father pointed an angry finger at him.

Buster saw Holly playing with her bubble maker. As she made bubble after bubble, he began to chase them.

He was popping all the bubbles.
He liked hearing them pop.

"I'm the bubble buster!" he shouted.

"Holly, can I have a turn?"

"As long as you don't break it!" said Holly.

Buster dipped the wire ring into the soapy water and blew into the circle. A stream of little bubbles came out. Next he made long, wobbly bubbles.

Then he wanted to blow square bubbles. He bent the ring into a square. The wire broke.

"Buster!" Holly cried and grabbed at him.

Surprised by Holly, Buster stepped back, slipped, and fell into the flower bed.

Uncle Fred had just put compost on the flower bed! Buster was covered in compost.

Holly felt like laughing and crying at the same time.

Uncle Fred held his nose. "Phew!
You stink!"

Dad sprayed Buster with the hose.
"Ahhh!" gasped Buster.
"Now take a shower," said his father.

CHAPTER 2

Buster and the Huge Bubble

In the shower, Buster made bubbles.
He used shampoo, soap, and some
bubble bath. He covered himself
in a sudsy suit of bubbles.

With his foot over the drain, the shower began to fill with water.

Buster stomped with his other foot to make more bubbles. Bubbles filled the shower. Water flooded out the door and across the lawn.

The bubbles joined together making a bigger and bigger bubble. Soon there was one huge bubble.

Buster was inside the huge bubble.

"Wow!" he yelled.

The bubble rose. A gust of wind sucked the bubble from the shower and out the door.

Buster's father ducked. Uncle Fred
stepped back and fell into the pool.

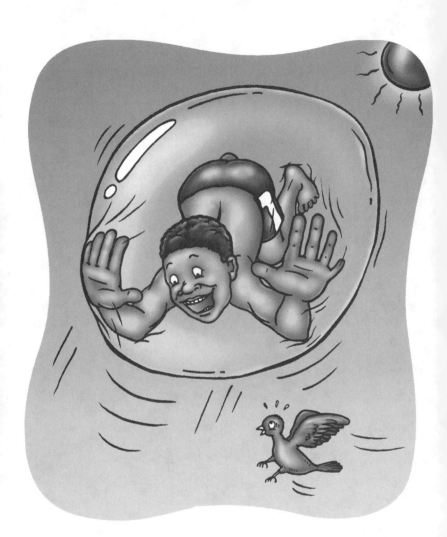

Out in the bright sunlight, the bubble began to rise.

Up, up, up it rose.

"Wow!" yelled Buster.

He could see Holly was amazed. As he rose, her face grew smaller and smaller.

Buster could see the whole yard.
Then he could see the whole street.

"Wow!" shouted Buster.

Buster was floating away. He could end up in outer space. He could end up on the moon. He could end up anywhere!

It was time for the Bubble Buster to take control.

He was about to burst the bubble
when he looked down. He was way
above a sea of rooftops.

"Oh no!" Buster moaned.

The bubble floated gently on. It passed over roads full of toy cars, toy people, and toy houses.

Buster was heading toward a giant smokestack. Smoke billowed from it. The bubble got black and sooty. It was hard to see where he was going.

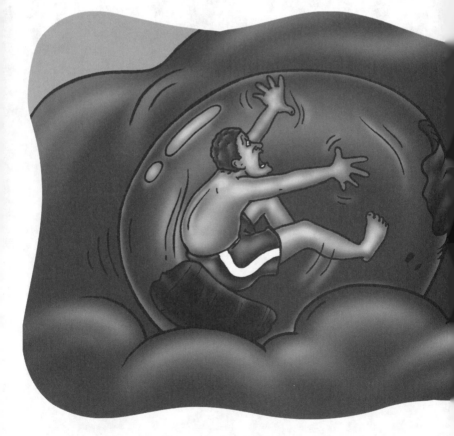

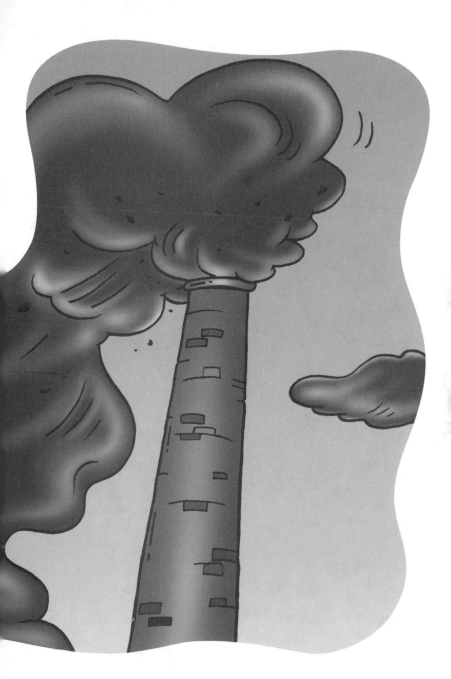

Buster leaned over to try to see. The bubble sagged and began to roll. Buster tumbled around as though he was in a clothes dryer.

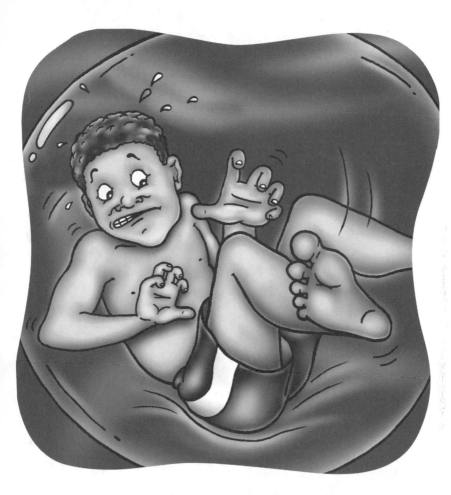

He was scared. He was so high.
What if he broke the bubble
with his foot?

The bubble slowed as it moved into some clear sky. Buster was glad to have left the soot and smoke behind.

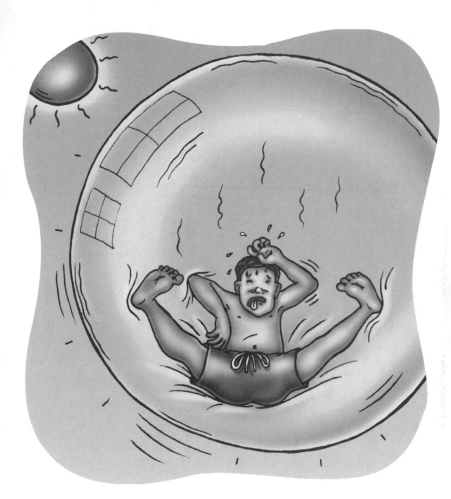

The afternoon sun made the bubble
hot inside. It was expanding. The
bubble's wall grew thinner, like a
balloon.

Buster began to sweat. The thin walls could barely hold him. He kept still. He kept very, very still.

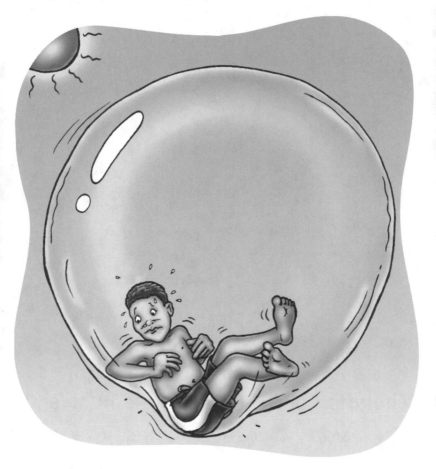

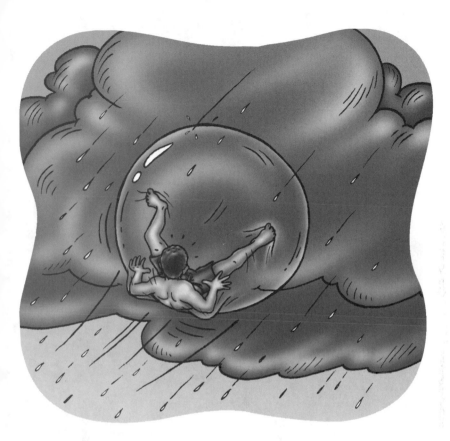

Suddenly, it was dark. The bubble was sucked up into a storm cloud, where it was cold. The bubble began to shrink.

Holly's Clever Idea

Night came. Wind caught Buster's bubble and moved it across the black sky. The cool air made him sink lower.

Now he was over a park. He could see sparkles of light below.

Maybe, they're having a party, Buster thought.

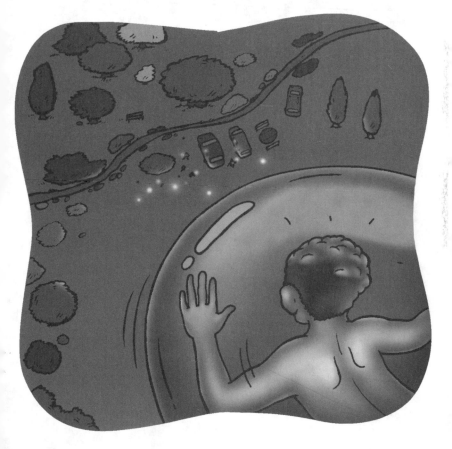

Suddenly, the night sky was full of fireworks. A rocket raced past. A shower of bright sparks lit the sky and fell to Earth.

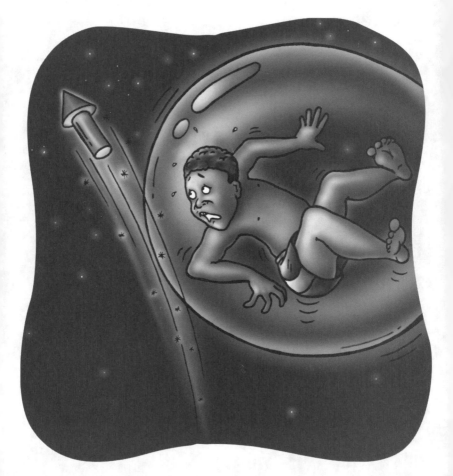

Two sparks shook the bubble. It was about to burst.

But the sparks just made the bubble spin, and it rolled away.

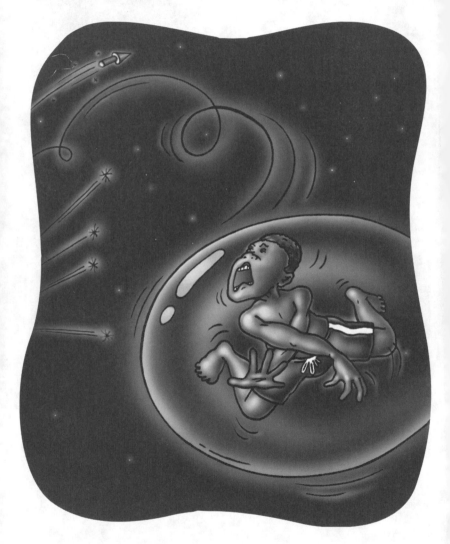

Buster tumbled and tumbled. The sky spun around him. He didn't know which way was home.

Buster huddled up and closed his eyes to stop the tears. He thought he would never see his father, Uncle Fred, or Holly ever again.

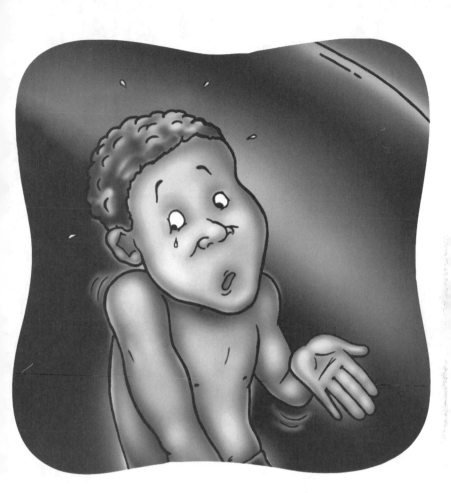

But Holly had figured out how
Buster could find his way home.

Buster opened his eyes. He could see a small light up ahead. It was Uncle Fred's swimming pool.

Holly had turned on the lights in the pool. She was sure Buster would see them. She was right.

Buster headed for the pool.

Holly threw a paper plate. It went flying up toward the bubble.

Its edge nicked the bubble.
The bubble burst!

Buster was falling. He thought he
was going to break every bone in his
body.

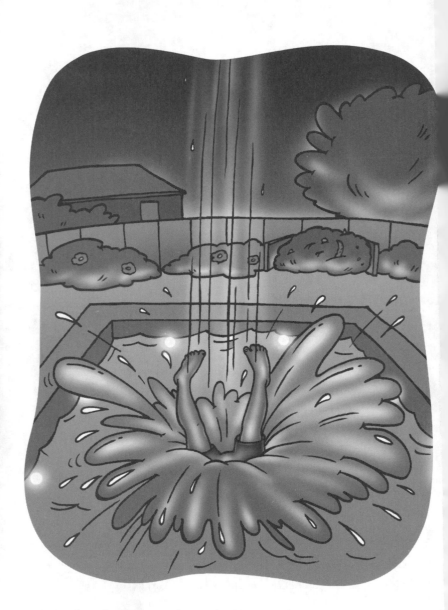

"Splash!" He landed in the pool.

Buster climbed out of the water. Uncle Fred put a towel around his shoulders. Buster turned to his sister and said, "Thanks, Holly. I owe you one."

GLOSSARY

 **billowed**
rolled out of a chimney

clothes dryer
a machine that
dries clothes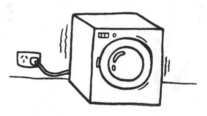

 **compost**
rotting food scraps
that make food
for the garden

expanding
getting bigger

moaned
made a sad,
low noise

sooty
black from smoke

tumbled
rolled about

Alan Horsfield

While relaxing in the bubble bath, Alan Horsfield got a bright idea for a story. He hopped out of the bath completely covered in bubbles and dashed to his computer. Unfortunately, someone left the door open, and he was whisked away by a gust of wind to Fiji and has never returned.

Luke Jurevicius

My parents told me that my first words were "ink jar," which I believe was the inspiration for my first masterpiece — a scribble on the kitchen wall. If only I had kept my first creation, perhaps one day it may have ended up in a museum. My latest project, *Bubble Buster*, was fantastic to illustrate, but I do confess I avoid the bubble bath and the sudsy soap, just in case.

Copyright © 2000 Sundance Publishing

Published by Sundance Publishing
P.O. Box 1326, 234 Taylor Street, Littleton, MA 01460

Copyright © text Alan Horsfield
Copyright © illustrations Luke Jurevicius

First published 1999 as Sparklers by
Blake Education, Locked Bag 2022, Glebe 2037, Australia
Exclusive United States Distribution: Sundance Publishing

ISBN 0-7608-4937-4

Printed in Canada